SBN 361 03486 5

Published 1976 by Purnell Books, Berkshire House,
Queen Street, Maidenhead, Berkshire
Made and printed in Great Britain by Purnell and Sons Limited,
Paulton (Bristol) and London
Reprinted 1977

RUPERT
and the Jumping Fish

Illustrated by Colin Smale
Based on an original story by Bestall

PURNELL

CHAPTER 1

One sunny day, Rupert wandered into the garden to find his father cutting away some long green shoots from the base of an old tree. Rupert offered to help, but Mr. Bear smiled and said, "I've got a much better idea. Why don't you choose one of these strong shoots, and find a pin that you can bend, then you can go fishing."

"What fun that would be, Daddy," cried Rupert. "I'll go and find a pin now."

He very quickly made a lovely rod, and borrowing some nylon twine from his Mummy, he hurried off eagerly to the river.

On the way the little bear was surprised to see a number of birds flying about excitedly over a spot near the river bank.

"I wonder what they can be looking at," he thought, as he took a short cut across a field to the river.

There, lying perfectly still on the river bank, was 'Rastus, the country mouse.

"Hello, 'Rastus," called Rupert, quite startling the little fellow. "What's going on here? I saw all the birds."

'Rastus went on gazing at the water and whispered, "There's a funny sort of fish just here, that seems to have come up from the

sea. It keeps jumping out of the water."

"My goodness!" interrupted Rupert, quite forgetting to keep his voice down, "I think I can see it! Look, just below the surface there!"

The two little pals held their breath and watched the tiny fish. But it didn't jump, and after a while 'Rastus got bored, and started off for home. Rupert was disappointed and was about to leave as well to find a quiet fishing spot, but just at that moment a bird on a branch overhead flapped its wings at Rupert, and chirped, "Rupert Bear, I have a message for you." Rupert looked up eagerly and the little bird puffed out his tiny breast with importance.

"That funny little fish has been calling your name every time he jumps. He asked me to fetch you."

The little bear was very puzzled by this piece of news, and frowning, he hurried back to the edge of the river bank to see what the strange fish could want. Then he realised that the poor fish was probably too scared to speak to him while he carried a fishing rod. Quickly Rupert hid the rod behind some bushes.

Suddenly, with a flash of green scales, a fish leapt out of the water and flopped onto the bank. A tiny gurgly voice whispered, "Please, are you Rupert Bear?"

Rupert smiled and nodded, feeling quite sorry for the poor little thing, which looked exhausted.

"Oh, I'm so glad I found you," gurgled the fish. "The sea-serpent is in great trouble, and he says that only you can help. Please go to Rocky Bay straight away, and I'll lead you to him."

Before Rupert could say a word, the worried little fish flopped back into the water with a noisy splash and was gone.

Just then, 'Rastus appeared at Rupert's side.

"I heard you talking to someone and came back to see who it was," he explained.

Rupert replied with a puzzled frown, "Well it's very queer. That fish wants me to help the sea-serpent. But I can't think how I can be of any use."

"Perhaps it's just a joke, Rupert," said 'Rastus, scratching his head thoughtfully.

"I don't think so," said Rupert. "That little fish looked really upset and he was exhausted by his long swim. I shall have to try and find out what's wrong. It might be something really serious."

"May I borrow your fishing rod, then, if you're not going to use it?" asked 'Rastus hopefully.

"Of course, but don't catch the little jumping fish by mistake. I must hurry," called Rupert, as he dashed away.

CHAPTER 2

Rupert ran all the way home, and panting out his story to Mrs. Bear, explained that he would have to go out again. Mrs. Bear smiled.

"Well run along, dear," she said, "but don't be late home for your tea."

Rupert rushed off, pleased that his Mummy had allowed him to go.

He took the quickest route he knew through the woods, to find Sailor Sam at his fishing hut.

Sam thought that Rupert's story sounded nonsense, but the little bear was so serious about it, that the kindly sailor said he would try to help, and brought his old skipper, Captain Binnacle, to hear the tale.

"Well, well," said the old salt, stroking his beard, "I really don't know what to make of your story, young bear. But if you really want to go to the serpents, I'll take you to Rocky Bay. From there it will be up to your friend the fish!"

"Oh, thank you," cried Rupert with great excitement. "I really do believe someone is in danger out at sea, and if I can help, I will."

Together, the two set off in Captain Binnacle's very old, rattly car, and soon Rupert glimpsed the blue sea beyond the rooftops of the fishing village.

"Nearly there," shouted Captain Binnacle, over the noise of the engine.

Rupert was beginning to thoroughly enjoy the ride, but remembering his mission he stood up eagerly to see if he could spot the fish.

"I'll take you to the headland," suggested

Captain Binnacle. "Your fish will most likely turn up there."

Rupert thanked the old sailor for his help, and set off over the rocks to the edge of the headland.

"If I stand up straight, the fish will be able to see me straight away," he thought.

But as he balanced on the slippery rocks, he was surprised to see another much bigger fish swimming straight towards him. Raising his head out of the waves, the fish asked, "Are you Rupert Bear?"

"Yes," replied Rupert.

"You must hurry," ordered the fish. "I will take you to the sea-serpent myself."

Rupert looked alarmed at this. "I can't swim very far you know," he said. "Perhaps we can find a boat?" he added hopefully.

The big fish looked very doubtful, but luckily two puffins who had been watching suddenly interrupted.

"Excuse us for saying so," said one, "but if it were a very little boat, the fish could pull it. Come with us."

Rupert scrambled over the rocks behind the two puffins and they soon flew down to a large rock. Behind it was the most enormous, perfect shell Rupert had ever seen.

"There you are, Rupert," said one of the puffins, proudly. "You won't find a better boat than that."

Rupert climbed into the shell.

"Well it certainly seems all right," he said with a smile. "Thank you, puffins."

Just as Rupert was climbing out of the boat, he spied Captain Binnacle clambering over the rocks towards him.

"There you are, little bear. I was just beginning to get a bit worried about you, as you had disappeared so soon," said he.

Rupert explained how the puffins had helped him find a boat.

"Do you think we can make this shell safe to ride in?" he asked the captain.

The old captain stared in astonishment.

"I must say you do get the strangest ideas, young Rupert," he said. "Still, I'll do what I can."

Quickly he strung some corks on a long rope, and tied them round the rim of the shell.

"There you are," he said. "Even if the shell does fill with water, it can't sink."

Rupert waded out a few yards into the water and towed his boat a little way to try it out.

-B

Suddenly the little jumping fish leapt out of the water, nearly toppling him over.

"That's marvellous," he piped. "I could even pull that along myself without any trouble!"

The tiny fish seized the ends of the cord in its mouth, and telling Rupert to jump in, set off towards the headland again. The old captain kept pace along the shore, almost as excited as Rupert himself.

The big fish was bustling anxiously to and fro there, and came swimming up to meet them.

"Right," said he. "We've got no time to waste. Let's be away. Hold on tightly, little bear, but don't be frightened, for although we'll be going very fast you'll be safe with me."

Waving a nervous goodbye to Captain Binnacle, Rupert settled himself in the bottom of the boat, holding tightly to the edge of the shell. With a splash, they were off.

Their tremendous speed quite took Rupert's breath away, but he hung on bravely, remembering the fish's words.

They bumped and crashed over the waves and Rupert realised that he'd never travelled

so fast in his life before. The water was very deep and green out here, and very soon the shoreline vanished and there was nothing around them except sea and sky.

He was just beginning to feel a tiny bit seasick when he sighted a small group of rocky islands ahead.

"This must be the home of the sea-serpents," thought Rupert with excitement.

CHAPTER 3

There seemed to be no sign of life amongst the rocks.

Rupert remembered that his Daddy had talked of these strange sea-monsters, which only a few sailors had seen. It was said that although they were quite alarming to see, they were really very shy and had never been known to harm anyone.

Rupert was still a bit scared, and as they sped through a rocky cleft into a small bay, he stared around him nervously.

"Don't worry, Rupert," said the little jumping fish kindly, "the sea-serpents will be so pleased to see you."

With this, he leapt onto a rock at the edge

of the water, and raising his head made a funny high pitched noise. Straight away a very long lithe creature emerged from beneath the surface, and clambered out onto a rock.

"Goodness me," thought Rupert. "This really is a very strange creature. I hope he is as friendly as everyone says. He looks very young although he is so big."

The young serpent seemed very relieved to see Rupert, and after talking quickly to the little jumping fish, he slithered off into the water and swam away at high speed.

"Don't worry, Rupert," said the little fish. "It won't be long now before you see what's wrong. That serpent has gone to fetch his Daddy."

In a short while the serpent returned. This time he had with him a very big old serpent.

"Ah, Rupert," said he in a gruff voice, "it's good of you to come. We are in great distress.

"Only a week ago I met a very friendly little person, and I brought him home as a new friend for my son. He doesn't seem at all well though, and we don't know what can be the matter. We thought you might be able to help, before it's too late."

Rupert looked puzzled. "But why send for me?" he asked.

The old serpent gave him a kindly smile.

"The little person knows you, as you'll see. He told me how clever you are and so I sent for you at once to make him better."

Before Rupert could reply, he was lifted

high into the air by the back of his jersey, and swiftly the serpent swam off, with Rupert firmly held. After a very speedy journey across the bay, Rupert was gently lowered onto some rocks

at the edge of a lagoon on another small island.

"There's my little pal," cried the young serpent, swimming quickly to a small group of rocks on the shore.

"Why, it's my friend the merboy!" said

Rupert in surprise and rushed over to the little fellow, who was lying quite still on the shore.

"What's wrong?" cried Rupert. "Have you got a pain?"

The little merboy could hardly speak, and Rupert had to kneel down to hear him.

"I'm so very weak," whispered the merboy. "I can't move and I can't swim. I think I might be going to die."

Rupert was very frightened to hear his little friend say this, and ran straight back to the rocks where the sea-serpents waited anxiously.

"I don't know what to do," he cried. "It's my friend the merboy, and he seems to be very ill. I've no idea what's the matter with him. Is there a mer-doctor anywhere who could save him?"

"Good gracious me!" said the big sea-serpent. "I didn't know there were such people! I shall set off at once and see if I can find one."

He swam off immediately and soon disappeared out to sea, leaving Rupert and the young serpent with the little merboy. The serpent gazed sadly at his sick friend.

"I can't leave him alone," he said. "He might die, and I couldn't bear that." Two big salty tears rolled down his cheeks.

Rupert felt quite sorry for him, and decided that the best thing he could do was to find some food.

"Cheer up," said he to the sorry-looking serpent. "There may still be some chance of saving our pal. I'll go and look for something he might eat, while you keep watch."

He set off through the undergrowth, bravely pushing aside the long vines and strange plants which brushed him as he passed. It was certainly a wonderful island, with beautiful flowers and strange bright coloured animals which darted in and out of the trees and bushes around him.

Suddenly he noticed a tree with dark blobs hanging in it. Rupert peered at them.

"Those look as if they might be a tasty kind of fruit," thought the little bear.

CHAPTER 4

Rupert was just about to try one of the blobs for himself, when he saw a parrot looking down at him.

"Do you think those things can be eaten?" called the little bear.

"Certainly," squawked the parrot. "I should say so. I'm over a hundred years old and I've lived on them all my life!"

Rupert quickly gathered as many as he could carry and set off through the wood again to the waiting serpent.

When he reached the shore, the little merboy hadn't moved, and lay still, looking very pale.

Rupert told the sea serpent of his find, but his friend didn't think it would be very suitable fare for an invalid.

"These are nuts, Rupert," he grunted. "I don't think the merboy is strong enough to crack them."

Rupert was very worried by this and gently shook the merboy.

"Do you think you could manage to eat a nut if I break it into small pieces for you?" he asked hopefully.

The poor little chap could only shake his head and whisper, "It's very kind of you, Rupert, but I've had plenty to eat. I don't think that can be the trouble." Straight away he fell into a deep sleep again.

"Oh dear," said Rupert. "What can be the matter with him?" The little serpent, who had been anxiously watching, shook his head in despair.

Rupert sat down gloomily to try and think of a solution, and at that moment the old serpent appeared looking very glum.

"Oh, have you found a mer-doctor?" cried Rupert. "The little merboy is looking terribly ill; he must have help soon, or it will be too late."

"It's no good, little bear," replied the serpent. "I've looked everywhere and there simply isn't a mer-doctor to be found. No-one has ever heard of one in these parts. You are our only hope now."

Rupert couldn't think what to do. He wandered off a little way, and thought hard to himself.

"The little merboy isn't hungry, therefore he can't be starving. Perhaps he is so weak because he is thirsty. This water looks lovely and clear. Perhaps it is good to drink as well."

He knelt down on a flat stone and cupping his hands drank from the lagoon.

Suddenly he jumped to his feet, and to the astonishment of the two serpents, started leaping about and shouting with excitement.

"I've got it, I've got it!" he cried. "I've got the answer!"

"I'm sure that is very satisfactory," said

the old serpent, with a puzzled stare, "but what in the world do you mean?"

Rupert couldn't wait to explain and scampered over to the merboy.

"You must get up and leave here as quickly as you can," he cried. "I've found your trouble. You live in salt water, and the water here is fresh water. You might have died if you had stayed here any longer. You must get to the sea. Come on!"

The poor little chap was far too weak to move though.

"Please, Rupert, do you think you could carry me?" whispered the tiny creature. "I'm not going to be able to get there on my own."

"Of course I will," replied Rupert, and he bravely lifted the little merboy onto his back.

They started the dangerous descent over the slippery rocks to the sea shore. Several times Rupert nearly fell on the perilous rocks, but at last they arrived at the water's edge.

Gently Rupert lowered the little fellow into the sea, and waited anxiously to see if he would recover.

"He seems to be a very long time under water," thought the little bear.

CHAPTER 5

Rupert breathed a sigh of relief, as the fair curly head suddenly emerged. The little merboy smiled and called, "Thank you, Rupert. You've saved my life. I feel much better already. I think I am going to be all right!"

To show Rupert that he was really better, he started to dive and frolic about, leaping and splashing until Rupert was drenched as well.

Laughing and chattering, the pair quite forgot the sea-serpents in their relief, until the little jumping fish arrived to see what all the noise was about.

"Why, Rupert, you've succeeded. How marvellous!" cried the little fish. Just then, the two sea-serpents swam up and exclaimed in amazement at Rupert's cleverness.

"Well done, Rupert," they said. "We knew you would be able to help."

"It was very bad of you to put a salt-water merboy into a fresh-water lagoon," replied Rupert, sternly. "He might have died, and I think you had better let him go home at once. Please fetch the shell boat."

The two serpents looked very bewildered and sheepish at this telling-off from such a

little bear. They had never been scolded before, but when they realised that he was quite right, they bowed their great heads and apologised for being so careless. Everyone agreed to be friends, and the two serpents were about to swim off for the shell boat, when the young one turned to his father and said, "Please, Daddy, can we make up for our bad behaviour by inviting Rupert and our little chum the merboy, to stay two more days with us? There is so much to see and do here in the islands, and I get so lonely playing by myself all day."

The old serpent's face lit up with a smile.

"That's a good idea, son," said he. "What do you think, Rupert?"

"Well, my Mummy and Daddy are expecting me back," said Rupert, "but if I could get a message to them somehow I am sure they would allow me to stay. Thank you very much for inviting me."

"It's no problem at all," piped up the little jumping fish. "If I set off now, I'll be in time to tell the story to your friend 'Rastus. I am sure he will explain to your Mummy and Daddy."

Rupert jumped up and down with excitement at the thought of the wonderful time ahead with his little friends, and gave some quick instructions to the tiny fish.

"Be sure to keep an eye open for the fishing rod," he said. 'Rastus knows you now, and I am certain he would not do you any harm, but try and warn him that you are coming."

The little fish looked a bit frightened, but then he perked up. "I'll take the big fish with me," he said. "He'll look after me." And off he swam.

CHAPTER 6

Rupert and the little merboy were both very hungry after all this excitement.

"Come with me," said the young serpent. "We'll prepare you a lovely meal of fresh sea fish. First, I will go and fetch the shell boat to carry Rupert."

The two chums chattered excitedly when he had gone.

Soon he returned with the shell, and with Rupert and the merboy on board, they set off across the bay. On the way the serpent explained that there were marvellous places to explore in the islands, and added that there was a family of sea-lions whom he would like Rupert to meet.

"You're famous, now, Rupert," he declared. "Everyone is talking about you and how clever you were to save the merboy's life."

They quickly arrived at a sandy beach. The serpent suggested that Rupert find some driftwood to build a fire. "You'll get cold," he explained, "while we two are all right in the water."

Rupert built a little fire and while the others were fishing, he dried his clothes out.

Then he went and collected some fruit and a few nuts from the edge of the forest.

Soon they were all sitting on the edge of the shore.

"I think I shall cook my fish," said the little bear. "I don't think I should like it raw."

He offered the serpent and the merboy some fruit, and they were surprised to discover that they enjoyed every mouthful.

The three friends spent a long time planning what they would do for the next two days and then the merboy and Rupert said goodnight to their host, and settled down to sleep in a dry cave amongst the rocks.

The next day was bright and windy and Rupert woke to find the waves sparkling in the breeze, and his little friend, now fully recovered, and playing at diving.

"I'll teach you to dive, Rupert," said he. "There are lots of lovely rocks and different coloured seaweeds under the water. Watch me!"

And with a flick of his tail he was gone. Rupert watched, laughing, as his cheery friend surfaced beside him with a splash.

"Don't be afraid. Take a deep breath, close your eyes and hold your nose, and I'll take you down."

Rupert did as he was told, and he felt the little merboy tug at his arm. All of a sudden they were standing on the sea bed.

"Open your eyes," said a bubbly voice beside him. Rupert opened one, then both

eyes, but remembered to hold his breath. It was a wonderful sight. Tiny fish danced around his head and seaweed swirled around interesting-looking caves and cracks in the rocks.

Rupert turned at the sound of a booming voice behind him. It was the young sea-serpent. The little bear was about to say that he looked much bigger under water, but remembered just in time not to open his mouth. So he pointed upwards and swam to the surface.

"I say, it's certainly strange down there," he said, shaking water everywhere. His friends joined him, and for a while they played water polo with a funny-looking gourd that the merboy had found on the beach.

"Come on," said the serpent. "Let's go and visit the sea-lions."

Once again, Rupert climbed aboard the shell, and soon they were speeding towards another small island across the bay. Rounding a headland, they came to a group of sheltered rocks.

"I can see some strange creatures basking on the rocks," cried Rupert to the merboy.

"They look odd, but they are very nice," called the serpent. "They are my friends, the sea-lions. If I ask them nicely I am sure they will give us a wonderful display of swimming and diving. They often give shows in the summer, on all the islands. They're very good."

Rupert and the merboy were fascinated to meet the sea-lion family. They did look very odd and whiskery, but they were very friendly creatures, and grunted happily at Rupert.

CHAPTER 7

The serpent quickly explained their visit. "Ah, yes, so you're the clever young fellow," exclaimed the eldest sea-lion.

"We heard all about your brave deed," he went on. "I think the islands owe you something in return for your kindness."

Here the serpent interrupted. "Excuse me, sir," said he. "I told Rupert about your summer displays. We would love to see one."

"Certainly, my friends," replied the old sea-lion. "Kindly sit on those rocks and you will be able to see better."

Rupert and his two chums scrambled onto

some flat rocks above a small cove, and watched as one by one the sea-lions flopped into the water.

There followed a breathtaking display of underwater swimming, aquabatics, diving and jumping.

"It's a pity bears can't swim like that," whispered Rupert to the merboy.

"Never mind, Rupert," he replied. "You can move about on land better than any of us."

When the sea-lions had completed their show and two encores, the friends waved goodbye and headed back across the bay to the serpents' island.

The next day it was time to return to Nutwood again. The big fish was harnessed to the boat, and Rupert and the little merboy thanked the young serpent for their stay.

"Are you ready?" called the fish, and the two pals were whisked away towards Rocky Bay.

Captain Binnacle was watching there for Rupert's safe return.

"Bless my soul," he cried. "You've brought a merboy back. You must let me keep that shell boat amongst my treasures, Rupert."

He gazed in awe at the little merboy as Rupert bid him farewell, and he swam away. The old captain and Rupert were soon on their way back to Nutwood in the captain's car, with Rupert pouring out the story of his adventures all the way home.

"Well, bless my soul," he kept saying. "Gracious me, Rupert. You do get up to some strange things."

And that evening, as Rupert sat down to a delicious tea of toast and crumpets, he related to his Mummy and Daddy everything that had happened from the moment he first saw the jumping fish.